I0570470

OTHER BOOKS IN THE WIFE-TO-BE SERIES

Wife Insurance
Wife Next Door
Wife for a Day
Wife with a Plan
Wife for the Crowd
Wife Envy
Wife Again
Wife.Edu

A WIFE-TO-BE NOVELLA

A'NDREA J. WILSON

Divine Garden Press

Wife without a Ring is a work of fiction. All incidents and dialogue, and all characters with the exception of some well-known historical figures and public figures are products of the author's imagination and are not to be construed as real. Where real life historical or public figures appear, the situations, incidents, and dialogues concerning those persons are entirely fictional and are not intended to depict actual events or to change the entirely fictional nature of the work. In all other retrospects, any resemblance to persons living or dead is entirely coincidental.

Wife without a Ring. Copyright ©2014 by A'ndrea J. Wilson. All Rights Reserved. No part of this book may be used or reproduced by any means without written permission from the author with the exception of brief quotations in printed reviews.

Published by Divine Garden Press, LLC
P.O. Box 371
Soperton, GA 30457
www.divinegardenpress.com

ISBN-13: 978-0692303788
ISBN-10: 0692303782

Cover Design & Interior Layout by Divine Lit Services
www.divinelit.com

Above all, love each other deeply, because love covers over a multitude of sins.

(I PETER 4:8, NIV)

Super Bowl Wishes & Engagement Ring Dreams

Some people are gifted to sing, write, or play a sport. I'm a natural when it comes to making people look good. Give me an ugly duckling, three hours, and $100, and I will transform the poor soul into a swan—head to toe. When it comes to beauty, I'm considered a triple threat because I have my cosmetology license, aesthetics license, and an Associate's degree in fashion merchandising. I can basically do your hair, nails, makeup, and pick out the perfect outfit for your body shape. I have all of these skill not because I'm driven or passionate about a career in beauty, but simply because I love being beautiful.

Due to my extensive background and experience in all things beauty, I work for Canton's department store as a Cosmetics Manager. Right now, I'm testing a new product at the CuteChicks makeup counter. We just got these new lip liners in that are supposed to change the color of lip gloss.

I apply a cotton candy colored lip liner to my employee's lips, followed by a clear lip gloss. Instantly, the clear gloss turns frosted pink. Satisfied with the look, I take a step back and admire my work.

"How does it look?" asks Delia, who is my best friend, employee, and guinea pig.

"I love it. I'll definitely be purchasing a few of these," I say before passing her a handheld mirror so that she can see it for herself.

Delia takes several seconds to check herself out in the mirror, then says, "I don't know how you apply lip liner so quickly and accurately, Shawna. It takes me twice the amount of time to do what you just did. You know you've got a gift. I don't know why you're ready to give it all up so easily."

I roll my eyes. This is the zillionth time in the last three days that Dalia has mentioned to me that she disagrees with my plans to pass up on an upper management promotion. "Yes, I've got skills, but I'd much rather spend my time catering to my future husband than being some beauty guru. Call me old fashioned, but I was created to be a wife," I say.

She puts down the mirror and stands up from the high stool she's been sitting on. "That doesn't mean that you can't have a career and use your amazing talents at the same time Stop being so old fashioned. You're only 28, not 82."

"That's exactly what having a career means. I don't want to be like all of these women out here who are stretched way too thin. Being a good wife and mother is a full-time job. I don't want to end up neglecting my family or my own well-being because I'm trying to have it all at once. That's why so many married women look tore up from the floor up."

She grunts. I know that she's frustrated with me, but I refuse to change who I am or my priorities.

"But the regional cosmetics manager promotion is major," she pleads. "Do you know how many people would die for a chance to move up to a position like that? Everyone who works here—that's how many. And they want you. All you have to do is say yes and you'd double your salary. This is a no-brainer. Take the job."

I start talking with my hands, which often happens when I'm trying to explain myself. "First, they have not offered me the job. They offered me an opportunity to interview for the job. Second, I don't want to agree to take on more responsibility, just to have to turn around and quit when Andy and I get married. It makes more sense to just stay where I am so I don't have to let anyone down."

"Whoa, let's back up for a second," she says, holding up her right hand and giving me the universal gesture for *stop*. "Since you are numbering your points, I'll give you the real breakdown. First, they are offering you the job. The interview is just protocol. Second, you and Andy aren't even engaged. You're a fool if you make career decisions based on a marriage that hasn't happened yet, and may never happen. As much as you like shopping, being pretty all of the time is costly. You have bills to pay and you could really use that extra money. Stop being silly and take the promotion."

Andy Tate is the love of my life. We've been seeing each other for nearly two years and we're a serious couple. Andy's a kicker for the Pittsburgh Steelers, and I am so ready to be a NFL wife. Why spend my time worrying about moving up the ladder at Canton's when I'll be married to a man who plays for the best team in the league? "Andy and I are getting married," I say, slightly offended that she doubts our relationship.

She sucks her teeth. "Has he proposed yet?"

She knows that he hasn't proposed yet. I hate when people ask questions when they already know the answer. "No," I say, then add, "but he will."

"When?"

"Soon," I say confidently. "We've been talking about the idea."

Cutting her eyes at me, she asks, "Has he been talking about it, or have you been talking about it?"

"Isn't that the same thing?"

"Not at all. Until he actually gets down on one knee, asks you to marry him, and puts a ring on your finger, there are no guarantees. You don't want to pass up on a secure position for one that's only a possibility."

I'm over Andy's house, tending to my man after his hard day of practice. He is icing his leg to relieve the soreness in his muscles while I give him a shoulder massage to help him relax.

"Mmm," he moans as he shuts his eyes and appreciates my magic fingers. "You sure you didn't go to school for massage therapy too?"

I smile and continue kneading his skin. "No. But aesthetics school did teach me some basic massage techniques. I'm glad you're enjoying it."

He lets out a deep breath. "Yes, I am. I don't know what I would do without you."

Aww. It's such a sweet thing for him to say. I swear I love this man. If only we were married . . .

"It will be like this all of the time once we get married," I say, dropping one of my "marry me" hints. It's something that I've found myself doing a lot lately.

He lets out another satisfied moan. "Yeah, you're right."

Did he say I was right? This is progress. Determined to get a proposal out of him, I probe for more. "So you agree that we should get married?"

He simply nods and says, "One day."

I can't help but feel disappointed. We've been together for two years and I still can't seem to get a solid "yes" out of him. It's not that I want him to say yes to me proposing to him because I'm not actually proposing, I'm just putting it out there. What I really want is for him to take the bait, buy me a ring, get down on one knee, and ask me the five most important words in the world—*Shawna, will you marry me?* Why is he making this so hard?

I decide to try a different approach. Maybe I'm spoiling him too much. Maybe I'm too available. Maybe if I told him about this promotion at work, reminding him that I could be somewhere else, he'll realize what's at stake.

"Well, my job is still hounding me about interviewing for that promotion," I say, watching his facial expression closely. "Honestly, I'd rather bypass it so that I can be available for you, but it would double my salary and give me a chance to travel more often for free. Personally, I could use the money considering I'm a single woman, living on my own, and having to take care of myself."

He doesn't even flinch. "I would love for you to be here with me too, but it sounds like a good opportunity for you. I wouldn't want to stand in your way. Maybe you should go for it. What can it hurt to at least do the interview?"

It could hurt a lot. If I get this job, it will force me to be away from him. Even the interview is in another state. "The interview is all the way in Miami. The job is being a regional cosmetics manager for the southeast region."

His eyes never open. "Miami's a fun city. Would you have to relocate?"

I'm pouting because he's not reacting. Why doesn't he get that getting this job would mean me spending time away from him? I try to tell the truth, but accentuate the travel aspect. "No, I can mainly work from home or the corporate office here in Pittsburgh, but I would have to travel quite a bit. I would need to visit the stores throughout my region several times a year."

"Sweet," he says likes he's happy for me—or about me leaving. "That sounds like a great deal. When do they want you to go to Miami for the interview?"

I roll my eyes and stop caressing his shoulders. He doesn't deserve my magic fingers. "In two weeks."

He smiles. "Really? I have a game against the Dolphins in two weeks. It would be great if we're there at the same time. We could meet up afterwards."

Okay, so this is a game changer. Andy's going to be in Miami and he wants me to be there when he's there. Maybe I'm being paranoid. Maybe he does want more with me. "You've got a game there? A Sunday game?"

"Yep."

I restart the massage. "I'm sure I could arrange it so that my interview is the Friday before your game day. That way I could be at your game."

He moans for the third time. "Make it happen, love."

Two weeks later, I'm at the Dolphin Mall in Miami, dressed for success in nothing but designer labels. My favorite color is pink, so I finish off my gray and white ensemble with a pair of pink pumps and pink accessories. The store manager has given me a tour of the location, and now I am meeting with the current regional cosmetics manager, who is about to retire, and the director of cosmetics, who would become my direct supervisor—should I take this position. Both ladies give me multiple compliments on my attire and natural beauty.

"You're just so adorable. That's what this company needs. Someone who is young and understands what makes a woman feel beautiful," Kim, the current regional cosmetics manager, says.

"I agree, Kim. Fresh blood will give us a new and hip perspective. Keeping up with Macy's, Nordstrom's, and Bloomingdale's isn't easy. And with a lot of these cosmetic companies starting to put their own stores inside malls, it's hurting our sales. We need them to want to sell their products at our counters, and we need customers to come to our stores first when they run out of their favorite mascara or foundation," Diana, the director of cosmetics, says.

"Thank you, ladies," I say. "I've found at my store that women like to get everything they need in one place, if possible. Why go from store to store if you don't have to? But often we shop around because of price and company reputation. And actually, we'll get over high pricing if the reputation is strong enough. No one complains about Coach's prices because it's Coach. In the case of companies like Coach, the price is what makes it desirable. It's the fact that everyone can't afford it."

"I'm going to cut to the chase," Diana says. "We like you, Shawna, and we want you in this position. We've been watching you for a while now, and we believe that you have what it takes to help Canton's increase our cosmetic sales. Usually, we don't have candidates your age that are so well-trained and ready for this kind of responsibility, but you are exactly what we're looking for. We're willing to offer you a significant salary increase, as well as a sign-on bonus. We're also willing to negotiate some of the perks of the job to meet your lifestyle needs. All you have to do is say yes, and the job is yours."

I look back and forth between the two women. Their faces are lit up with excitement and anticipation. I have to admit, the job is very appealing, but I wonder how it will affect my long-term plans of marriage and family. It's crazy how the very thing I want most, I can't seem to latch on to, but the things I couldn't care less about, come easily and without asking. So much of this decision is dependent on my future with Andy, so it's difficult to make a choice without his feedback.

"Thank you for the offer," I say. "Would it be alright if I take a few days to think it over?"

"Pardon my asking, but what is there to think about? You already work for the company. We're basically offering you more money to do many of the things you're already doing," Kim says.

I don't want to insult them so I choose my words carefully. "I understand, and I'm truly grateful for the opportunity. It's just that I'm planning to get married soon and I really need to discuss this with my significant other."

"That's fine. Of course we can give you a few days to think it over," Diana says.

"Aren't you dating some football player?" Kim asks.

"Yes."

"I didn't know you were engaged. And to a professional football player?" Diana inquires.

Although I'm uncomfortable sharing too much of my personal life with these women, I brought Andy into the conversation, so I'll have to explain. "Well, technically we're not engaged yet, but we're talking about it. I just want to get his feedback since the position will require a bit of traveling for me."

"It sounds like you're going to make a good wife. Maybe had I consulted with my ex-husband about some of my plans, we'd still be married," Diana says. "Do what you have to do and get back to us by Tuesday with your decision."

Sunday afternoon I attend the Steelers vs. the Dolphins game. I have the pleasure of sitting with a few of the other players' wives. I've seen them around, but since I don't want to look like a groupie, I typically don't come to too many games. I'm surprised that the ladies greet me and let me socialize with them. There's Melanie who is married to the quarterback, Jake Oaks. She has a few children so she only goes to the major games like the playoffs and Super Bowl, but she also attends when there's an away game somewhere exciting, like Miami.

Then there's Karima. She's married to a running back, Lionel Scott. She's at every game, front and center, afraid some woman will try to sink her paws into her man. Finally, there's Natasha. She's married to a tight end, Ronald Rainey. I think she only comes to show off whatever new item she has purchased since the last game.

"So, Shawna. I'm kind of surprised to see you here. You never come to games, especially away games. Are things getting serious between you and Andy? You guys have been together for some years. I'd thought you'd be married by now," Natasha says, being nosy.

"I guess I'm not into football as much as you all are. I'm actually in town for a job interview," I say, purposely ignoring her question about my relationship status.

"Girl, when your man plays pro football, you play the game too. If you're planning a life with Andy, you better get used to being here, or another woman will be waiting on the sidelines for him," Karima says.

"You said you're here for a job? Are you planning to move to Miami? How'd the interview go?" Melanie asks.

I appreciate the change of topic. "The interview went well," I say. "They offered me the position. No, I'm not moving, I'll just have to travel a little if I take it."

"What kind of job is it?" Melanie probes.

I feel a little awkward talking to these women about my job. None of them are employed, so telling them I work at the mall sounds a bit juvenile. I want to be where they are—living off my husband's income while I hold down the home-front. I try to formulate my response in a way that doesn't make me sound as broke as I really am. "I currently work as a cosmetics manager for a department store. This new job is to oversee the cosmetics department of all of the stores in the southwest region. So basically it would be taking what I do for one store and doing it for about fifty stores. Of course, there would be someone local who does the daily tasks, but I would supervise him or her and make sure they are meeting their quota."

Melanie's eyes light up. "That sounds so interesting. I wish I had a career, but raising three kids and keeping up with Jake is more than enough. There's no time for anything else."

"I think that's why I like you," Karima says to me. "You're not like these other wanna-be-NFL-wives. You can fend for yourself and aren't looking for a payday from Andy."

I almost mention to her that Lionel's her payday, but I decide to keep my smart comments to myself. I want to be accepted by these women, especially if I marry into the league.

"So are you going to take the job?" Natasha asks.

I shrug. "I haven't decided yet. It's an excellent offer, but I need to talk to Andy about it before I make a decision."

The women glance at each other and laugh.

"You're going to ask Andy if you should take the job when you don't have to? You two aren't even married yet and you're already allowing him to choose what's best for your life? You're definitely ready to be an NFL wife," Melanie concludes.

A Nightmare Near Ocean Drive

Andy and I, along with a few other players and their wives, hang out in South Beach. The guys are pumped after beating the Dolphins, 31-14. Dating a football player, I've become accustomed to people looking at us and asking for autographs periodically, but being with the other players intensifies the public reaction. Men and women alike swarm us, begging for an autograph, a touch, a moment with the famous athletes. I pay attention to how the wives stay stuck to their men, daring any female fan to get too flirtatious. As much as I love the energy of the group, I wonder if I'm truly ready for the demands of being a wife to a celebrity. I believe that I am, but seeing these women play their roles so well makes me worry that I'll cave under the pressure.

Upon finishing an expensive meal at one of the restaurants on Ocean Drive—which Jake the quarterback paid for—we all get into a club for free and are escorted to VIP. Andy and I aren't much of party goers, so after a couple rounds of champagne—for celebration purposes—Andy and I catch a cab to my hotel. Canton's is covering all of my travel expenses, so they have me staying at the Four

Seasons Hotel downtown. Andy, being a gentlemen, walks me to my room. When we get there, I expect him to give me a kiss and leave, but he lingers for a little. Since he is staying for a while, I decide it's a good time to talk to him about the job offer.

"They offered me the job," I say as he takes a seat on the sofa in my suite.

He smiles brightly at me. "That's wonderful. Congratulations. When do you start?"

I take a seat next to him. "I haven't given them a yes or no yet."

"Why not?"

"I just wanted to talk with you about it first."

He sighs. "You don't need my permission to take a job, Shawna."

I want him to understand me. I need him to know that my future is with him, but for some reason, he always seems so aloof about us. "I know, but you're such a big part of my life, and I don't want to make any major decisions without considering how our relationship might be impacted," I say then reach out and touch his bicep. "They'll want me to travel and take on more responsibility. It could mean being away from you from time to time. Are you okay with that?"

He plants a kiss on my forehead. "Babe, if this is what you want, and if it will make you happy, I'm happy for you."

I feel like screaming. I've been trying to be subtle, but it's not working. I'll have to take the direct approach. "Andy, I know you're a very supportive boyfriend, and I love that about you, but I'm thinking about us right now, not just me. I want us to get married and have a family, and if this job is going to get in the way of that, then it won't make me happy. I'm only happy when I'm with you."

He stares at me for a second which makes me nervous. I can tell he's thinking, but I can't discern if his thoughts are positive or negative. Have I pushed to hard?

"So, you really want us to get married?" he asks.

I nod, a bit worried. "Yes."

He pauses for a few seconds then leans back on the sofa and says, "Okay."

I'm confused. "Okay what?"

"Let's get married."

What? "Are you serious?"

He grabs my right hand and kisses the backside of it. "Yeah. We've been together for a while, and we have a good relationship. We make each other happy, so why not?"

As much as I'm ecstatic that he's finally agreeing to marry me, I'm also disappointed that there's no big to-do about it. "So, is this a proposal?"

He shrugs nonchalantly. "I guess you could call it that. I don't have a ring or anything, but all that's not really necessary to agree to get married. Right?"

Yes, a ring is necessary! I feel like crying, but I manage to say, "I guess not."

He turns his body toward mine. "So what do you say? Are we getting married or not?"

This is the worst proposal in the history of proposals. No ring, no get down on one knee, no romance, nothing! But I love him and I want to be with him, so I say, "Yeah . . . yes. Of course I want to marry you."

He smiles, satisfied with himself. "Cool. When I get back to Pittsburgh, I'll talk to my accountant about getting you a ring."

So he'll get me a ring in a few days. I can live with that, right? "Okay," I say.

He stands up and yawns. "I'm getting tired, so I'm going to head back to my hotel."

Believe it or not, I'm actually glad he's leaving. I need time to think, and most likely, cry. "Okay. Wait. Andy? What about the job? Should I still take it?"

He nods. "I think you should. I'm getting older and I'm not going to be in the league for much longer. It wouldn't hurt to have you bringing in some additional income once we're married."

I offer him a bittersweet smile. "Okay."

"I'll see you back in PA. Love you," he says before kissing me and walking out the door.

I spend my Sunday night—the night I finally got engaged—bawling my eyes out.

Chicken Salad Sandwiches & Other Things I Now Hate

I return to work on Tuesday in a solemn mood. The moment Delia sees me walking past the Fashion Fair display, she leaves her post at the CuteChicks counter to greet me.

"I've been trying to call you since Sunday. Why haven't you returned my calls? I thought you were lying in a dumpster somewhere in Miami," she says, overly dramatic.

I sigh. I'd seen her countless calls because I intentionally forwarded them to voicemail. I love my best friend, but I'm embarrassed about Andy's weak proposal and the fact that I have nothing to show for it. "No dumpster, I've just been preoccupied."

She looks at me—no actually, through me. "Did something happen while you were in Miami? Was it the interview? Did it go poorly? I could have sworn they were going to hire you."

Delia's upset because she thinks I didn't get the job. She's clueless to what's really going on, and it's all my fault. I want to confide in her, but Delia is a bit of a drama queen and I really don't want her making the matter worse than it already is.

I decide to try to pacify her with the news about the job. "The interview went fine. They offered me the job, right there on the spot."

She jumps up and down for joy. "I knew it! I knew it." Bringing her enthusiasm down a notch, she peers at me suspiciously. "Did you turn it down?"

I laugh at her lack of faith in me. The laugh feels good considering the fact that I've been crying for the past thirty-six hours. "No, I called them this morning and accepted it. I'll be transitioning into my new role at the end of the month."

She grabs me and pulls me into her arms for a hug. "That is so wonderful. I'm so happy for you!"

When she lets me go, I run my hands along my skirt suit to smooth out any creases she may have caused. "Thanks," I say without much passion.

Obviously, she notices my indifference and calls me on it. Putting her right hand on her hip, she says, "Okay, something is definitely wrong. The interview went well, you're taking the job, but you haven't called me in days, and your attitude is gloomy. What's really going on? Is it Andy? Did you two break-up?"

"We're still together," I answer, hopping she'll let it go. She doesn't.

"He did something to you, didn't he? Don't make me have to go looking for him."

This is why I don't want to tell her the full story right now. Delia is one of those women that will hype you up and have you arguing with the man you love or something trivial. She calls it being honest. I call it being too opinionated. If I tell her about Andy, she'll dog him out for being an idiot, and then tell me to either make him give me a ring or dump him. I want to be with Andy, so neither option will do.

I rehearse my words in my head, trying to figure out the best way to tell her about the engagement without lying, but without telling the whole truth. "Calm down. No need to mess up your makeup. He didn't do anything. It's not anything like that," I say.

She glares at me. "Then tell me what's up."

I muster up a big smile and put my left hand behind my back. "We've decided to get married."

Her eyes widen. "Really? Wow. Well, that's good news. That's what you wanted, right?"

Thinking about what I wanted and what actually happened causes my smile to turn into a frown. "Yes, it's good news," I say, despite not feeling the good part of it.

"Okay, so cheer up and let me see this ring. With all of the money he's making, I know he had to get you at least a 2-carat rock."

Leaving my hand behind my back, I say, "It was sort of an impulsive decision, so we're going to pick out the ring later this week."

She nods, accepting my excuse. "Okay, I can feel that. Make sure you go with him; that way you can get something you really like. You said you guys were going to get married and now it's actually happening.

And he proposed in Miami. Now that's romantic. So, how did he do it?"

"Do what?" I ask to avoid having to actually answer the question.

She looks at me as if I've completely lost my mind. "Propose. How did he propose? I'm surprised that I even have to ask you all of these questions. I thought if he ever popped the question that you would be calling me in the middle of the night with all of the details, not me having to interrogate you just to get the story."

This is harder than I thought it would be. I hate being dishonest with her, but Delia isn't the kind to be brushed off. I realize that she's going to hound me about it until I divulge the not-so-romantic story to her, which I'm just not ready to do. "I'm sorry, Delia," I say. "I don't mean to be so vague. I'm just a bit jetlagged from the trip and overwhelmed by all of these changes in my life. Please don't take it personally. Once I get some rest, I'll tell you everything."

She lets out an annoyed huff and walks off toward her counter. Looking back, she says, "I'm going to hold you to that."

I bet she will.

It's evening and Andy shows up at my cozy, two-bedroom apartment, unannounced.

"I have a bit of bad news," he says as he walks inside, kisses me on the forehead, and makes himself comfortable in my kitchen. He opens the refrigerator door and pulls out a container with chicken salad that I made early this morning.

I feel my body tense up. *Is he backing out on me now?* Worried, I ask, "What? You don't want to marry me anymore?"

"Why would you say something like that? Of course, I want to marry you. Don't even think that," he says as he grabs a loaf of bread and starts making himself a sandwich.

I watch him, thinking about whether or not I should help him, but I'm too emotional to morph into my usual Betty Crocker mode.

"Sorry. I'm just a little . . . What's the bad news?"

He adds a large pile of potato chips to his plate and sits down at the kitchen table to eat. "I talked to my accountant today and he's suggesting that I hold off with any major purchases or financial decisions until I see whether or not the Steelers renew my contract. That means I won't be able to get you a ring right away. We'll also have to put off any wedding plans for a few months. I won't be able to commit to a date or details until I know what my income is going to be after this season." He takes a bite of the sandwich.

I'm standing there, watching him merrily eat while I look and feel like a fool. I didn't think this proposal could get worse, but somehow, it has. "I don't understand. Don't you have a bunch of money saved up?"

He eats a few chips, then says, "Yes, but most of that is for retirement. My career is not like others. I only get to play football for a limited number of years. Once I stop playing, I'll either have to find another career or I'll have to live off the money I've saved up. Thankfully, when I joined the league, I took the advice of a more seasoned player, got a trustworthy accountant, and saved quite a bit of my money versus spending it all on useless stuff, like most players do. We'll be well off financially if I don't get another contract, so don't worry. But since I'm really not sure what will be my next career move, I need to continue being smart about how I handle my money, at least until I know if I'm still going to be playing next year."

I want to cry, but I hold it together. Not only do I not have an engagement ring, but my NFL fiancé may be getting cut from the team? This can't be my life. "But you're their kicker. They need you. That back-up kicker is a joke. They can't replace you with him."

He is enjoying his food as if all is perfect in the world, while I die a slow and painful death. He shrugs at my last comment. "They could always trade me, or bring in someone from another team. The NFL is a very unpredictable employer. I've been with the Steelers the majority of my career which is rare. Most players get moved around a lot, then eventually cut. I'm hoping they give me at least another 2-year contract, and then I'll quit once that ends. My agent believes he can negotiate it, but there are no promises."

"Why didn't you tell me all of this before?"

He gets up and heads back to the fridge. Taking out a can of soda, he opens it and gulps down about half of it, then places the can on the table. He sits back down, ready to resume his meal. "Because it wasn't anything for you to worry about. The only reason I'm telling you now is because we're planning to get married and I'll have to wait a little while before I can get you a ring, but that doesn't change anything for us. We're still going to get married and we're still engaged. Have you told anyone yet?"

I don't want to tell anyone. I don't have a ring or an exciting proposal story to tell. "Just Delia," I say.

He chews and swallows another piece of the sandwich, then says, "You haven't told your folks yet? I told my mom yesterday. She was very excited. She's been trying to get me to settle down and give her grandchildren since I was 21. She'll finally get her wish."

I wince. "You told your mom?"

"Yeah. I actually told several people. The whole team knows."

I gasp. "The entire Pittsburgh Steelers football team knows that we're engaged?"

His face is smug and I really don't understand why. He hasn't done anything to feel proud of. He didn't even get down on one knee.

"Yeah. Everyone's excited. They're throwing us an engagement party this Friday night at Jake's house.

Nothing extravagant, just the players and their wives or girlfriends."

I am completely and utterly embarrassed. "Oh my gosh. This is a nightmare."

"I'd thought you'd be thrilled about it," he says, then takes another swig of the soda.

I am mortified and he doesn't get it, not even a little. "How can I go in front of all of these people without a ring?"

He gives me a blank stare like I'm being irrational. "These are my teammates. They don't care about all of that."

"Maybe your teammates don't care, but their wives will care. And I care."

He gets up and comes over to me, wrapping his arms around me. It feels good to have him hold me, but that doesn't change how horrible I feel.

"Babe," he says, "I know that you want a ring, and I'm going to get you one, a really nice one. I just can't do it right now. At this moment, I could only spend about a thousand or two, and I know that you're going to want something a little fancier than what $2,000 can buy."

"You can't get it on credit or something?" I ask, nearly pleading.

He places his finger under my chin and turns my face toward him. "Come on, Shawna. You and I both know that credit is worse than cash. I'll end up paying two to three times the amount in the end. It's just best for us to wait until we know what's what, and then I can give you whichever ring you want—within reason. We'll set a budget that we both can agree upon and we can go shopping together. I promise that as long as you pick out a ring that falls under the maximum amount of the budget, I'll buy it for you—cash. No loans, no debt. The ring will belong to you, not the bank. Will you just give me a little time?"

"Fine," I say, caving in. What else can I do but wait? I just hope no one notices my empty ring finger.

Stalker Moments

Unfortunately, by Thursday, someone does notice my empty finger—Delia. Due to having to complete all sorts of paperwork for the new position and several pre-scheduled meetings, I didn't go back to the store on Wednesday. She's persistent and called me a few times, but I allowed her calls to rollover to voicemail. She even tried to get slick on me and called my mom who, without missing a beat, called me. I also sent my mother's call to voicemail, knowing I'll never hear the end of it when I finally call her back. I don't even listen to her message because I know it's nothing but a long rant, ending with, "And you better call me back!" Why can't people respect my desire to not talk to them?

Now it's Thursday, and I can no longer run from Delia. As expected, she pounces on me the moment she sees me getting out of my car in the mall parking lot. I wonder if she has been waiting inside her car for me to arrive, but I hate to assume my best friend is a stalker.

"There you are!" she says as she runs over to me. "If I wasn't your best friend, and if we hadn't known each other since elementary school, I would defriend you on Facebook and never speak to you again."

She's really mad at me. Delia doesn't believe in removing anyone from her Facebook friends list, even the people she doesn't like. I don't get it, but she says she keeps them on her list so that she can have a front row seat when their lives fall apart. If she has considered removing me from her Facebook friends list, I've really offended her.

"What did I do?" I ask, feigning innocence.

Her eyes narrow. "Don't play games with me, Shawna Claxton. You *know* what you did. Sending my calls to voicemail, avoiding me for three days, not even taking your momma's calls. Does any of this sound vaguely familiar to you?"

The jig is up—not that I ever had a chance to fool Delia. "Vaguely."

She looks me up and down critically. "Um hmm. I thought so. So what gives? Why aren't you answering my calls . . . and why don't you have a ring yet? I thought Andy was taking you ring shopping this week."

I sigh. "You and me both."

"The week is almost over. Are you going this weekend? Is he backing out of the proposal or something? Don't make me have to go down to Heinz Field."

"No, he's not backing out."

She stomps her foot on the ground. It's her way of letting me know that she's fed up. "What's going on,

Shawna? You're not being forthcoming with me and I'm tired of racking my brain about your unusual behavior. Tell me now or I'm going to call Andy and find out what's really going on."

My eyes widen. She wouldn't. Yes, she would. I actually met Andy through Delia—that's how she has his phone number. A little over two years ago, Andy was out one night and lost his wallet. Delia—a saint on her good days—turned his wallet in at Heinz Field since there was information inside it saying who he was and where he worked. Andy was so appreciative that he gave her two season passes and invited her to dinner, which she took me along. He said that she'd saved him a bunch of time, money, and hassle by returning the wallet, so he wanted to show his deep gratitude. At the time, Delia was dating this guy named Junior—of course, that wasn't his real name, but that's what everyone called him. I was surprised she took me with her instead of Junior, but she said that she thought Andy and I might make a cute couple. She was right. Sparks flew at dinner, he and I exchanged numbers, and we've been together ever since.

If Delia calls Andy, he'll think I've stooped so low as to turn my friend loose on him. He'll think I'm being immature and petty about the ring issue. He might even call off the engagement. What's more horrific than not having a ring is not having Andy at all.

"Wait," I say, frantically. "Please don't call Andy. You'll only make it worse."

She stabs me in the shoulder with her index finger. "Don't make me pop you upside the head. What in the world is going on? Did you lie about the engagement?"

"No, it's true," I say reluctantly. "We are engaged but . . ."

"Spit it out."

I throw my hands up in surrender. "The whole thing is a mess. He didn't really propose to me. We were out in South Beach after the game, having a good time. Then he went with me back to my hotel room, and we were talking about the job offer. I mentioned that I cared about how the job would impact our relationship because I wanted to marry him, and then he's like, 'Okay. Do you really want to marry me? Let's do it then. Let's get married.' I didn't know what to say because he was finally agreeing to marriage, but there was no real proposal; it was more like a business agreement."

She shakes her head and laughs. "That's sounds just like Andy. All business."

"But that's not the end of it," I whine. "He says he'll get me a ring when we get back to Pennsylvania, but then, he talks to his accountant and they decide he needs to hold off on any major purchases until he finds out whether or not he's going to get released from the team at the end of the season."

She looks concerned, but the moment she opens her mouth, I find out it's not for the reason I want her to be. "Andy's getting cut?"

I really don't want to discuss my bootleg fiancé's football career when I'm in the middle of my own crisis, yet I oblige her with a response. "No. Maybe. He doesn't know. His contract expires this year so his agent is negotiating with the team. But there's a real concern that they may not renew. He could go to another team, but he won't. He'll just retire. He doesn't want to move around and he's planning to retire in two years anyway. But that's beside the point. The point is that I'm engaged without a ring. How can I tell people when I have no proof? The ring is the proof; it validates the engagement. This is like being a wife without a wedding ring—it doesn't make sense."

She gives me a blank stare—the same stare that Andy gave me just a couple of days ago. "There are plenty of married people who don't have or wear their wedding rings."

"Yes, eventually people may stop wearing them or lose them, but everyone has one at the beginning. It's so vital to being married, it's even written in the ceremony. With this ring, I thee wed." I can't believe that I actually have to explain myself to my best friend. She should just get it. Matter-of-fact, every woman should get this. Who really wants to be engaged without a ring?

Delia obviously must be one of the few women in the world that are okay with having a ring-less, left ring finger because she has the audacity to say, "I'm sure you'll have a ring soon, at least by the time you two get married. Don't you think you're blowing this out-of-proportion? And you call me the dramatic one."

I want to strangle the woman. She has forced me to talk about the problem, and now wants to dismiss it. "I'm blowing it out-of-proportion? Delia, you wouldn't talk to Junior for a month after he forgot your birthday. I have a right to be upset."

She twists her lips. "Why do you have to bring up old stuff? You know I don't like to even remember that jerk's name."

It was low for me to throw her ex in her face, but I'm stressed and not much like myself at all. "Sorry for dredging up the past," I say, earnestly. "I'm just surprised that you aren't on my side."

"I'm always on your side; you're my best friend," she says, lightly nudging me with her elbow. "But that doesn't mean that I always have to agree with you. The way I see it, you want to marry Andy and now he's agreed to take that step with you. Just appreciate the progress and stop getting caught up in the technicalities."

I consider her words. Maybe she's right; maybe I should focus more on the fact that I'm finally engaged to the man I love. "I'll try," I say. I want to be more rational about the situation, but I'm not going to lie to myself. I want a ring, and until I get one, it will be difficult for me to share the engagement with others because I know they'll instantly check out my hand. I feel stuck between a rock and a hard place.

"So, what's next? Have you set a date?" she asks calmly, signifying her anger with me has receded.

"He says we can't plan anything until we have a better idea about his football career. I really hope they give him an idea about what they intend to do sooner rather than later," I say. "Oh, the quarterback is throwing us a casual engagement party at his house tomorrow. Just the team and their spouses."

"Really? Awe man. I want to come, but I've got to work closing tomorrow night and then open on Saturday. There's no way I'll make it to work on time if I hang out with you all Friday night."

"I'm sure there will be a real engagement party once Andy gets his finances straight, and you can help me plan it," I say in an attempt to make her feel better.

"I can live with that," she says. "Have you talked to your mom yet? She was pretty upset with you about not telling her about the engagement."

Just when I was starting to chill out about my engagement fiasco, Delia hits me with another harsh dose of reality. "You told my mom?" I sort of ask-scream at her.

Our emotions have switched. Now I'm the livid one and she knows it. She cowers a bit and says, "Yeah, but I thought she already knew. You haven't called her back yet?"

I groan. I understand it was an honest mistake on her part, but Delia may have just ordered my execution. My mother, Janice Claxton, doesn't like to be ignored by anyone, and she especially doesn't like to be left in the dark. I'm sure that she'll kill me the moment she tracks me down. "No. I've been preoccupied with the whole job thing and dealing with Andy. I haven't had the chance," I say in my defense.

Delia lets out a sarcastic laugh. "You had the chance; you just didn't want to hear her mouth."

I nod. "That too."

We've been standing outside talking for over ten minutes and our clock-in time is nearing. I look down at my watch, and as if understanding my cue, we both start walking toward the store's employee entrance.

"Are you going to call her?" Delia asks. "It's been a couple of days. She is really going to flip out on you."

I sigh. I don't want to deal with the woman who gave me birth, but it's inevitable. "Don't remind me. Yes, I'll give her a call. On Saturday."

A Thief in the Night

"**M**om! What are you doing here?"

To my horror, Janice Claxton barges into my apartment at ten o'clock Thursday night without ringing the doorbell or knocking. When I first moved into the apartment years ago, I'd given her a key for emergency purposes only. Until this point, she's never used her key without getting my permission. Now, she is standing in my bedroom, hovering over me like a thief in the night, scaring the pants off me.

I make a mental note to either take back her key or change the locks ASAP.

She places both of her hands on her hips and I know a lecture is sure to follow. "Shawna Marie Claxton! I can't believe that you would go off and get engaged in another state and not have the decency to tell your mother."

"Mom, I—"

I start to explain, but she interrupts me. "And then, bring your sorry tail back to Pennsylvania and ignore my phone calls like I'm some bill collector. You should be ashamed of yourself."

"I was going to—"

Cutting me off again, she says, "I don't want to hear the excuses because there is no excuse for this kind of behavior. I raised you better than that. Now, get your tail out of that bed and tell me what in heaven's name is going on with you."

I cautiously slide from under my warm blankets and walk over to her like a scolded little child. With my eyes looking down on the carpeted floor, I say, "I'm sorry, Mom. I wasn't trying to disrespect you. I've just been going through a lot of changes lately."

I peer up at her quickly to see if her demeanor has changed. It hasn't.

"Continue," she demands.

I take a deep breath and attempt to tell her enough to pacify her, but not overshare. My mother gets animated about the smallest issues, and I really don't want to spend the rest of the night trying to calm her down. "I went to Miami for a job interview, not to get engaged. I didn't know it was going to happen. Andy had a game, so it worked out that we were both there at the same time. And it wasn't a *real* proposal anyway."

She cocks her head to the side. "What in the world is a *real* proposal? Did he ask you to marry him or not?"

"Not exactly. We sort of agreed that we should get married."

She folds her hands in front of her. "Well it sounds like you're engaged to me. Why didn't you call and tell me? Does his momma know about it? I'm sure she does."

"Yes, he told his mother," I say, then quickly add, "Please don't be offended, Mom. I haven't told anyone."

She sucks her teeth. "You told Delia; that's someone."

"Only because Delia forced it out of me. You know how she is. She wouldn't leave me alone about it."

My mother exhales and shakes her head at me as if disappointed. "I just don't understand you. You go on and on all of the time about wanting to get married and wanting to be a wife. Now, you're finally engaged and you're keeping it a secret. What's the matter? Is it that you don't love Andy?"

I walk over to my bed and collapse on it. I think I am handling my mother well thus far, but it is very draining. "Of course I love Andy. It's not that. I'm just a little embarrassed about the way it happened. I didn't get the whole down on one knee, give me a big ring thing." I'm exhausted and the words spill out before I've had time to edit them in my mind. Upon realizing what I've just said, I sit up quickly and cover my mouth. Just when I thought I was out of the fire, I've leapt into the frying pan.

My mother's eyes widen in surprise. She instantly looks down at my hand, which I try to hide, but it's too late. My mother is more materialistic than I am. She will definitely have a problem with me not having a ring, hence the reason I've kept it from her. "Wait. He didn't give you a ring? All that money he's making and he's too cheap to give my baby a ring?"

"It's not like that, Mom," I say in Andy's defense. "The whole moment was just unplanned so he didn't have a ring at the time, but he's is going to get me one."

She looks at me unconvinced. "When?"

"Soon," I lie. "We're going to go pick it out together. This all happened less than a week ago. I'm trying to transition into a new job, and he has football practice, and then his team is throwing us an engagement party. There's just a lot going on right now."

Her hands return back to her hips, which is not a good sign. "What's this new job all about? And why wasn't I told about this engagement party? See, this is what I'm talking about. You've completely kept me out of the loop."

The only way I'm going to get out of this mess alive is if I play up to her ego. The Bible says to agree with your adversary quickly—so that's what I do. "You're right and I'm sorry. I wasn't going to even interview for the job, but Andy thought it was a good idea. The job is working as a regional cosmetics manager. Basically, what I'm doing now, but overseeing a bunch of stores in a different region. I'll officially start next month. I should have mentioned it to you, but I really didn't know if I would accept the offer, so I just wanted to keep it to myself until I made a decision.

"And I had nothing to do with the engagement party. A few of his teammates are throwing it at one of their houses. Not a big deal; it's only for the team. I just found out about it a couple of days ago."

I watch my mother as she mulls over what I've just told her. She wants to continue being upset with me. She likes to rant and rave. I know this because I've had a front row seat to her verbal fits my entire life. Since my brother and I have grown-up and left our parents' home, I almost feel bad for my father who's the only one remaining to put up with her outbursts. Then again, he married her so that's what he signed up for.

Her chest deflates and I know she's tapped out. Good. I am too.

I look over at my alarm clock and realize that we've been doing this mother-daughter dance for thirty minutes. I've got a busy day tomorrow with the engagement party in the evening. I need something new to wear and I must get my hair done. There's no way that I'm going to show up as Andy's new fiancée and not look like the most fabulous woman in the room. Since I won't have a ring to flaunt, I'll have to distract the group with my beauty, which is difficult to do in a room full of pretty women.

I glance at my mother. She's watching me, so I know she has seen me look at the time.

"Alright," she finally says. "It's getting late, so I'll let you go back to bed. I'm sure your father is probably wondering where I am."

I climb back under my blankets. "Thank you. Please tell Daddy I said hi."

She picks up her purse, which I had not noticed was laying on the foot of my bed. She begins to walk toward the door, then turns back before she makes it to the doorjamb. "With all of the excitement, I forgot to tell you that your Aunt Wanda sends her congratulations."

I gasp. Am I in the Twilight Zone? The last person in the world that I want to know about this engagement is Motor-mouth Aunt Wanda. "Aunt Wanda knows? You told her?"

"I most certainly did," my mother says. "It's not every day that I get to shut her up about that daughter of hers. I'm so sick of hearing Vanessa this and Vanessa that. Well, she almost turned green with envy when I told her that my daughter was engaged to a pro football player. You better hurry up and go ring shopping because I told her your diamond was twice as big as the one Vanessa's husband got her."

I moan. This cannot be my life. "Mom, how could you say that? You hadn't even seen my ring. Technically, you still haven't."

Not only do I have the pressure of my mom and the entire Pittsburgh Steelers football team on my shoulders over a proposal that didn't happen in the storybook fashion like I desperately wanted and needed, I now have to compete with my cousin's engagement ring. And let's not forget that Andy is trying to be cost-conscious when it comes to getting me a ring that I might not see for months!

My mom shrugs at my distress. "Andy is making at least a million dollars a year. I figure he would definitely outdo Vanessa's $400,000 a year surgeon. Tell Andy that you need at least four carats. Anything less won't do."

Liar, Liar

By **6:00 p.m. on Friday**, I look as if I just stepped off a fashion show runway in Milan. I take a personal day off from work and spend the entire day getting plucked, primped, and colored so that I can be the star at my own shindig—and not be outshined by one of the NFL wives. Two hours alone today are spent searching high and low for the right cocktail dress to wear. My attire has to be glamorous, yet not too dressy, simple, yet high fashion, and amazing, yet affordable. I'm not officially a league dependent and my wallet is nowhere as deep as theirs. While I am certain that some of them will be wearing hundreds and possibly thousands of dollars on their backs, I have to make $78.49 appear just as dazzling—and that's on clearance.

Andy picks me up from my apartment and ogles me instantly. I smile because I process his reaction to mean my day long beauty regimen was a success. Yes, this is the man who loves me, but he's seen me a zillion times. That's what regular looking people don't understand. When you date someone super-hot, over time, you get used to their looks. They're still attractive, but it's not the same excitement as it was when you first met them. Every once in a while the beautiful one must change up their look or do something special just to get a rouse out of you. This is the case with Andy. He sees me all of the time, so he doesn't act wowed by me anymore. Yet, here and there, I like to turn up the volume on my splendor and remind him of why I am the best choice—like tonight.

We get to the home of Jake and Melanie Oaks by 7:00 p.m. Oh course, they live in a swanky subdivision of an upper-class neighborhood outside of the Pittsburgh city limits. Both their subdivision and their house are gated, so we have to go through the security process twice to get in. Expensive cars line the long driveway of Jake's home and I begin to feel knots in my stomach. *Am I ready for this? Can I do this?* I look down at my hands, which I've adorned with a few gold rings that I own, making sure not to wear any jewelry on my ring finger. I hope that the other rings distract from the fact that I don't have an actual engagement ring. I hope my form-fitting red dress and red bottom heels distract from the fact that I don't have an actual engagement ring. I hope that my flawless make-up, long, spirally hair, and new strawberry-blonde highlights distract from the fact that I don't have an actual engagement ring. I hope. I hope. I hope.

The moment we walk into the front door, everyone begins to cheer. I assume that we were purposely asked to come to the party slightly later than everyone else so that we could have the red carpet treatment— literally. A velvety looking red carpet extends from the front door, through the foyer, and into the great room. Along with the applause, I see a few cameras flash and I hear his teammates begin to chant his last name. "Tate! Tate! Tate!"

I look up at the double winding stairway and there's a banner hanging from the second floor landing that reads CONGRATULATIONS TEAM TATE. The sentiment makes me want to cry. This is how you throw an engagement party. This is worth telling the story over and over again, unlike the way Andy sort of proposed.

Hand-in-hand, we walk the red carpet into the great room and are seated in two oversized chairs fit for a king and queen. For a moment, I forget all about my ring crisis and indulge in being treated like royalty. Guests begin to form a line near us, and couple by couple, they walk over to us, offering their congratulations and well wishes. By the time we've shaken hands with everyone, I am starving. The Oaks have hired caterers who bring us various hors d'oeuvres, as well as champagne. We soak up the pampering, tasting everything that comes our way.

Eventually, a few of Andy's teammates come over to us and want the inside scoop.

"So Shawna," one of them says to me, "how did our boy Andy pop the question?"

I am loving the party until this very second. Andy looks at me with a grin as he's waiting for me to tell them this Disney-like story filled with unexpected wooing and a heartwarming proposal. I freeze, not knowing what to say. I'm afraid that if I speak, I'll say something so negative that it will ruin the entire evening. I guess Andy must see the resistance in my eyes because after I don't immediately begin to brag, he does it for me.

"Don't let her fool you all. She isn't shy," Andy says. "But our proposal wasn't a bunch of unnecessary glitz and glam. You fellas know how I am—practical and to the point."

"You sound like you clubbed her over the head, threw her body over your shoulders, and announced, 'You my wife,'" one of the players joked.

That would have been better than what he did, I thought.

Andy laughed along with the men. "I'll have to remember that when you finally propose to your girl. I'm sure that will be exactly how you do it."

The guy nods and chuckles. "You know me, man."

"But all kidding aside," Andy says, grabbing my hand closest to him, "this is a very special woman. She's been a wonderful girlfriend to me, and I'm looking forward to spending the rest of my life with her. When you find someone like this, you have to keep her close."

Aww. That was really sweet. I look into Andy's eyes and think loving thoughts.

Andy kisses my hand then continues. "I'd heard her talking about marriage, but you know, during the season, my mind is so fixed on football that I wasn't considering what we needed to do as a couple. After the Miami game, it just felt right. I had my woman by my side, we had just beat the Dolphins on their field, then we go down to South Beach and the locals showed us so much love. I wanted every day to feel like that. I know I can't have a winning football game every day or even hang out in South Beach, but I can have every day with this gorgeous woman right here."

"Wow, dude. She's got your nose wide open," the same player joked and the rest of them began to laugh.

I think about what Andy just said and I can't help but feel mixed emotions. On one hand, his story is beautiful and I'm so glad that he feels the way he does about me. Yet on the other hand, his story is too beautiful and nothing like my experience on that day. Yes, I had a great time on South Beach with the team, and up until the moment that he agreed to marry me, it was a magical night. However, saying "Okay, let's get married," is not the same as deciding to marry someone and giving her a romantic proposal. Andy's version of the incident is completely skewed and doesn't reflect what really happened. For the sake of saving face in front of the crowd, it's a great tale, but

I feel cheated that our proposal wasn't as sweet as he just made it sound.

It is then that I realize that Andy and I live in two different realities. He really believes that his proposal was a good one that he should feel proud of, while for me, even replaying the moment in my mind gives me a headache. How could two people have two completely opposite ideas about what occurred on that night in Florida?

I continue to smile at the guys huddled around us, but inside I'm annoyed. The conversation among the men shifts to the upcoming game against the Baltimore Ravens and I take that as my signal to go to the bathroom. I don't mind football talk, but with the way I'm feeling, I'd rather take a breather from my fiancé and calm my nerves.

I spend a few minutes in the bathroom checking my makeup and hair, the typical stuff women do when we go to the bathroom in a group, except I'm alone. When I walk out, the Cheetah Girls are waiting for me—they're all wearing some form of animal print tonight.

"There's our new inductee," Natasha says. Today she has on a new diamond tennis bracelet. I'm jealous.

"Enjoying your party?" Melanie asks.

"Yes. We really appreciate you and Jake for opening up your home to us," I say as I try to walk past them without seeming rude.

"Looks like you'll be coming to more of the games," Karima says before taking a gulp from the champagne flute in her hand.

"When I can," I say. "With the new job, I'm not sure how much I'll be available."

I want to keep the small talk to a minimum. As much as I'm grateful for the engagement party, I still haven't figured out the angle of these three women. Do they really like me? Are they interested in bringing me into their circle? Or are they setting me up to tear me apart? Until I can trust them, I'd rather not play their game.

"Excuse me, ladies. I'm going to go check on Andy," I say as a curtesy so that it won't look like I'm running off.

"Where's your ring?" Natasha asks candidly.

This is what I was worried about. Although the men never question my lack of an engagement ring, the women notice and mention it quickly.

"What ring?" I ask, pretending to be aloof.

"Your engagement ring. This is an engagement party for you and Andy, right? So why don't you have a big rock on your hand if he proposed to you?" Natasha says.

My face feels hot. All three women are glaring at me, waiting for my response. I'm so embarrassed that I want to leave the party at this very minute, with or without Andy, but that would just make the matter more complicated.

"Natasha, leave the woman alone," Melanie finally says, coming to my defense. "Everyone isn't as materialistic as you. Just because you feel the need to show off your jewelry every chance you get doesn't mean Shawna has to."

"But who doesn't show off their engagement ring?" Karima asks. "Especially when they first get it. They've been engaged for a week. For about a month I wouldn't even take mine off before showering. I did everything with that ring on. I couldn't believe I was wearing that much money on one finger."

"My point exactly," Natasha says.

So much for letting Melanie stick up for me. After Natasha and Karima's line of reasoning, Melanie hops back on their side and peers at me, seeming perplexed.

"Uh," I say, searching for a good excuse. I've been so upset about not having a ring that I haven't taken the time to come up with a good lie for when people question me about it. "It needs to be resized."

Good one, Shawna. I wish I could give myself a pat on the back for coming up with a clever excuse on the spot, but that would make me look weird. "Yeah," I continue. "Andy miscalculated my ring size and it's way too big. I'm scared to wear it because it keeps slipping off and I really don't want to lose it. When he gets a chance, he's going to have it resized for me, but until then, no ring."

The women back off, thank God. They nod and change the subject, satisfied with my answer. Although I want to walk away, I stand there and chat with them for about fifteen minutes. Once I'm married, I don't intend to be at every game or event, but I will need to stay in the know and these women certainly know what's going on with the team both on and off the field.

"Did you hear that Paul and Rita split up?"

"You know, the IRS is auditing Jacob."

"Coach fined Tommy $1,000 for walking off the field during practice."

I am amazed at the amount of information about other people these women are able to retain and share. I can only imagine how they will be talking about me and Andy if they're not already doing so.

I excuse myself and head back over to Andy. The men are still talking about football, but I decide I'd rather hear about last week's stats than purposeless gossip. As I retake my seat next to my man, I observe a few of the players checking me out. I'm flattered. No one wants someone that no one else wants. My theory is as long as Andy's teammates think I'm hot, he will be sure to keep me close. As expected, Andy gently grabs my arm and pulls me a bit closer to him. Men. They're so territorial.

By 11:00 p.m., Andy's dropping me back off at my apartment. I'm dog tired, so I skip showering and washing off my make-up, and instead, simply throw on my pajamas and get into bed. I try to watch a movie on the Hallmark channel, but within minutes, I'm sleep.

I have Saturday off and plan to sleep in until noon or so, but my cell phone ringing wakes me up at 9:00 a.m.

"What?" I answer, having looked at the caller-ID and knowing it's Delia.

"Guess who made the front page of the *Pittsburgh Star*? You and Andy!" she screams into the phone.

I sit straight up in my bed. Oh no! Please God, say it isn't so.

Paparazzi Princess

I pinch myself to make sure I'm not still asleep and dreaming the words that I've just heard my best friend say to me.

"Ouch!" I whine as I feel the impact of my too rough squeeze on my forearm.

"What are you doing over there?" Delia asks.

I sigh. "Pinching myself. I had to make sure this is real. It's real, isn't it?"

"Yes, it's real," she says excitedly. "You and Andy are the cover story. There's a big picture of you two from your engagement party last night. The headline is TATE TAKES A BRIDE."

I let out a groan. "How did they get that picture? There were only football players and their wives or girlfriends there—no one else. Someone at the party must have sold us out."

"My money is on the girlfriends."

Lying back down and rolling over in my bed, I say, "I can't believe this is happening. Why me?" I think about the situation for a moment, then say, "You don't even read the tabloids. How did you even find that?"

"I stopped by the grocery store this morning to pick up a few things and while I'm at the register, I see my friend's face plastered across the magazine. I had to pick up a few copies."

"A few copies? Really, Delia?"

She giggles. I'm glad someone thinks my life is funny since I don't.

"Well, just in case you or your mother wanted one."

If she was in my presence, I would bop her over the head with one of those copies. "Mm hmm. What does the article say?"

"I'll read it to you. *Pittsburgh Steelers Kicker Andy Tate is officially off the market. After two years of courtship, he and his girlfriend, Makeup Artist Shawna Claxton, are engaged and planning a summer wedding. A close friend of the couple claims that Andy popped the question in Miami, Florida a week ago following the Steelers victory over the Dolphins, which Andy earned the team six points with two successful field goals. Upon return to Pittsburgh, Quarterback Jake Oaks congratulated the couple by offering up his suburban mansion for a team-only engagement party, which was held there Friday evening. Although the couple appeared attached at the hip, rumors are circulating as to why the bride-to-be wasn't wearing her engagement ring. Our sources tell us that the original ring purchased for Claxton was too big and needed to be resized. Based on Tate's 1.2 million dollar annual salary, we're expecting Claxton's ring to be the talk of the town."*

It had to be the Cheetah Girls. "Those backstabbing skanks!"

"Who?"

It was probably Natasha. She's the nosiest one out of the three of them, and she's the one who seems most interested in money. I can't believe I let her use me like this. "A few of the wives cornered me last night and asked about my ring," I say to Delia. "I may have led them to believe that it was being resized. Now, not even 24 hours later, this paper is reporting the same thing I told them. What did they do? Call the paparazzi from the party? Text message the picture as soon as they snapped it? I knew they couldn't be trusted."

"So you lied to a few women at the party, and now all of Pittsburgh believes Andy's already bought you a ring that's at some jewelry stores somewhere being resized? What are you going to do?"

Being in a difficult place, the last question I want to answer is, *What are you going to do?* If I knew what I was going to do, I would be doing it at this very minute instead of talking to my friend who I know is enjoying this theatrical occurrence in my life.

Irritated, I say, "What can I do? It's a tabloid so the information doesn't have to be true. There's no way that I can buy all of the copies of that magazine in Pittsburgh, so I guess I'll hide in my apartment for the next two days and hope that by the time I emerge on Monday either no one else has seen it or they've forgotten."

"What about Andy? What do you think he'll say when he sees it?"

I forgot about Andy. It's not that I really forgot Andy, I just forgot to think about his reaction. He can't blame me or think it's my fault. There's so much in the story that isn't true. Yes, I lied to the football wives about the ring being resized, but other things that I didn't say are also being reported making it easier for me to deny it all. I never mentioned a wedding date or anything about getting married in the summer. And it was Andy who told his teammates that we got engaged in Miami after the game, not me.

"More than likely Andy hasn't seen or heard about the magazine article yet. It's probably best if I'm the one who tells him first. If he finds out from someone else, there's no telling how much more the story might become slanted than it already is." Considering the idea of contacting Andy and letting him know about the article annoys me more. I let out a huff and say, "Why can't people just mind their own business?"

"Because they have no business of their own to mind, so they rather be all up in yours," Delia says with conviction in her voice.

Delia has to get to work soon, so we end our call and I head for the comfort of a long, hot shower. Thirty minutes later, as I think about the truth of Delia's words about others not having business of their own, I pick up my phone and dial Andy's number to fill him in on our citywide fame.

Fake It Until You Make It

"**H**ave you heard?"

I hear the clinking sound of weights hitting the floor and I instantly know Andy's at the gym.

"Heard what?" he asks, slightly winded.

I sit back on my sofa and prepare to give him the bad news. "I guess that's a no. Babe, we've got a little situation."

"Oh, Lord. What's going on?"

"Delia called me and told me that our picture is on the front cover of the *Pittsburgh Star*."

He gets quiet for a moment, then asks, "Really? For what?"

I look up at the ceiling as I talk to him as if the answers to all of his questions—and my own—are written across it. "Apparently, someone at the party last night sent them a picture of us and told them all about our engagement; however, they made up a bunch of details since they have no clue about us."

He exhales loudly. "What'd it say?"

I close my eyes before telling him this part. I really don't want to mention the ring, but if I don't share it with him, someone else will and he'll wonder why I left it out. "That we'd gotten engaged in Miami and were planning a summer wedding. It also talked about your salary and how I wasn't wearing a ring because it was being resized."

"I understand reporting the news and all, but where do these tabloids get off making up the details of our lives? I wonder who fed them that story." His tone is fairly calm, but I can sense that he isn't too happy about the article.

I have to maintain my innocence, so I say, "Personally, I think it was one of the wives or girlfriends. A few of them tracked me down last night and tried to pump me for information. But you know me. I didn't trust them, so I was pretty vague."

He lets out another heavy sigh. "Well, don't worry about it, Shawna. I knew the word would spread pretty quickly; I just didn't think it would end up in the tabloids. It'll blow over within a few days."

Maybe the story would blow over in a few days for Andy, but for me, the story has just begun. I hang up with Andy and within fifteen minutes, my phone is ringing again. I'm making a fresh fruit and veggie smoothie when I hear the buzz of the phone, and because my Bluetooth is still in my ear from my conversation with Andy, I hit the ON button without looking at the screen of my phone to see who's calling. I automatically assume the caller is Andy or Delia, but when my mother's voice pierces my ear, I regret answering without screening the call.

"So, how's my little superstar?" she greets me.

Oh no. I know that tone of voice. She's either seen or heard about the article.

I guess I'll have to be just as fake as her. "Hi, Mom. What's up?"

"Guess what I'm holding?" she asks with anticipation in her voice.

"I don't know." Yes, I do. "What?"

"A copy of today's *Pittsburgh Star*."

Does everyone in Allegheny County read this trash?

"That's nice, Mom. I didn't think you were the tabloids type."

"I'm not. But when your Aunt Wanda called me this morning practically screaming about your picture being on the front cover, I had to go out and pick up several copies."

Why does everyone in this town need multiple copies of this issue? If they keep it up, the *Pittsburgh Star* is going to purposely start following me and Andy around, reporting everything we do for the sake of increased sales.

"Oh, yeah, that. Delia told me all about it. It's just rumors. With Andy being in the NFL, stories like this are bound to happen. We both know about it and have blown it off." Why am I getting so good at lying?

I should go to church tomorrow morning. I'm in seriously need to repent.

She giggles. "Well I'm tickled pink about this story. Your aunt can't believe your luck. She wants to see you right away."

I tense up. "Why?"

"Because she says that she has to see it with her own eyes to believe it. The family's having dinner at my house next Sunday at three o'clock. Bring Andy if you can."

Thank God for Sunday football games, especially the away games. "Andy has games every Sunday. He'll be out of town," I say quickly and merrily. I hope his game will get us both off the hook.

"No worries. You can come by yourself," she says conclusively.

The verdict is in. Andy's off the hook, but I'm not.

I know there's no point in arguing with her or making up excuses. Neither my mother nor Aunt Wanda will let this matter rest until they see me in person. If I put off next Sunday's dinner, they'll just plan another one—when Andy can come. The last thing I need right now is Andy sitting across the dinner table from Thelma and Louise, being interrogated and eventually kidnapped for more information.

"Okay, Mom," I say with a lack of enthusiasm.

"And Shawna," my mother says before I can end our call, "be sure you have that ring on your finger when we see you. I'll just die if you step into this house bare-handed."

Thanks for laying it on thick, Mom.

For a week, I feel nothing but continued stress. Everyone in Metro Pittsburgh has read the stupid article on me and Andy. I'm tired of the phone calls, emails, text messages, and overwhelming new friend requests on Facebook. People who know me come up to me with a copy of the magazine in their hands and ask me to autograph it. Seriously?

By Saturday, I'm still dreading the idea of going to my parent's house for dinner. It's bad enough that my mother and Aunt Wanda will be playing tit-for-tat, but they're both expecting me to being wearing a very big ring that I don't have yet. With so much on my mind, I head to my favorite mall to do some retail therapy. There's nothing like buying something new to give me a change of attitude. I spend a few hours browsing and picking up a couple new pairs of shoes from Macy's. On my way out the door, I notice their costume jewelry section and check out the faux trinkets. I am stopped dead in my tracks by a beautiful, princess cut shaped silver ring with a large cubic zirconium that could easily be mistaken for a diamond. Immediately, a wicked thought enters my mind that I cannot shake—buy the ring and wear it to the dinner tomorrow.

Although I haven't previously considered wearing a fake ring, the idea is somewhat brilliant. No, it's not what I prefer to do, but it will get my mother and aunt off my back until Andy offers me my real diamond. I pick up the ring and slide it onto my ring finger. A perfect fit. I admire the way it sparkles against the store's lighting and makes my entire hand glow. I'm in love with this ring and it's not even authentic.

Quickly, I pull the ring off my finger and pick up its box. Turning the box over, I find out that the ring is only $20. It's a steal and I've got to have it. I tuck the ring back inside its box and head straight for the register. Crisis diverted. I can now go to the family dinner tomorrow with my head held high.

Flawless

I walk into my parents' house fashionably late at 3:45 p.m. The family never eats on time, and I don't want to have to spend any extra time there. Arriving forty-five minutes late ensures me that the food will be ready and everyone will either be already eating or eyeing the meal. To my disappointment, I'm the guest of honor and the family waits until I get there to bring the food out to the dining room table.

The moment I walk in, a hush falls over the living room and everyone stares at me. I like being the life of the party, not being in the spotlight, so I awkwardly step inside and offer a generic greeting to everyone at once. My mother rushes into the room with a bright smile on her face. I see her eyes dart toward my left hand that is proudly sporting the faux ring. Although I know the cubic zirconia will be difficult to differentiate from a real diamond, I begin to feel paranoid. *What if someone blows my cover?* Nervously, I rub my thumb along the cheap jewel and say a silent prayer that no one in my family is a gem expert.

"She's here!" my mother announces. "We can finally eat."

My relatives stand up. I can tell they're hungry and probably a little salty at me for making them wait. I think about apologizing, but how was I supposed to know that dinner was contingent upon my arrival. There are about a dozen of my extended family members in attendance, including my mother's siblings and several cousins. Of course, Wanda and her daughter, Vanessa, are present, both of them looking at me with contempt expressions. *What did I ever do to them?* My mother is creating enemies for me without my participation or approval.

"Before we pray over this meal," my mother says, "I want to thank you all for coming over to celebrate a very special time for this family. As you all know, I only have two children. My son is serving our country in the Army, and is currently overseas. We must continue to pray for him and his safety as he defends our freedom."

A few of the older family members nod and offer verbal agreements.

"And my daughter has just gotten engaged to Andy Tate, who you all know is the kicker for the Steelers. I'm so proud of her for finding such a good man to settle down with. I know he's going to take good care of my baby." She grabs my left hand and puts in up in the air for everyone to get a good look.

"He's already given her this gorgeous diamond ring. It's so flawless, isn't it?"

Flawless. That's the very same thing I thought to myself when I purchased it for twenty bucks at the mall yesterday.

A few "oohs" are heard from the family. I'm embarrassed for being put on display by my mother, but I knew before I came here that she would make a spectacle of me and herself. That's just who Janice Claxton is.

Aunt Wanda, no longer able to contain herself, hurries over to me and pulls my hand toward her face for closer inspection. Vanessa continues to hold up the wall, looking unimpressed. After ten seconds of eyeing my jewelry, Aunt Wanda lets out a "humph" and waddles back over to her daughter, whispering in the ear of the younger version of herself. Both of the women cut their eyes at me and my mother, which my mother takes to mean she's won this battle between the sisters.

"I almost forgot," my mother says, gloating. "Shawna also just got promoted at her job. She's now the regional director at Canton's."

What? My mother is really embellishing now, and Wanda and Vanessa are stewing.

"I'm actually a regional cosmetics manager," I say quickly before jealously bubbles over and burns down my parents' house.

"Stop being so modest. We're all very proud of you," my mother says.

Thank God for my level-headed father for stepping in and bringing my mother's antics to an end. "We are proud of you, Shawna, but we're also hungry and ready to eat. If you would all bow your heads, I'll lead us in a word of prayer and then we can dig in to this delicious meal."

Thank God for Russell Claxton. He's always been my hero, and he's always been there to save the day. Unfortunately, my hero can only do so much. God, save me from my mother and myself.

Busted!

After dinner with the family, I go directly home and take off the fake ring. As much as I think it's a terrific piece of jewelry, I refuse to wear it again until after Andy gets me a real ring. I can't chance the wrong person seeing me with it and the word getting back to my fiancé. By Friday, my work week has gone well, as expected. People have moved on past the engagement news and are now treating me like a regular person again. It's my last week in my old position, and the store manager throws me a farewell party in the employee break room. As much as it's somewhat exciting to be moving on to a new opportunity, I'm also sad that I won't get to see the team of people I've become accustomed to working with during my time at this Canton's store. I drop a few sentimental tears when the staff gives me a gold watch as a gift and an oversized greeting card with all of their names signed on it.

I am scheduled to fly down to Miami again on Monday evening. I've already completed the HR paperwork, so I'm ready to jump into training.

On Saturday, a loud banging on my door jars me from my midday nap. My rest is peaceful, until the knocking forces me up and to my front door. I yank the door open with fury, ready to give a well-deserved tongue lashing to whoever is on the other side.

Andy doesn't greet me with a hello or kiss like he usually does. Instead, he pushes pass me, entering my place without being invited. I close the door behind him, follow him through the foyer, and watch him in concern as he paces back and forth in my living room. He has some sort of paper rolled up in his hand, but I can't tell what it is.

"What's up, Andy?" I ask, completely baffled about his behavior.

He looks at me, agitated. Seemingly forcing a calmed tone, he says, "Shawna, I need you to be totally honest with me, okay?"

"Okay," I say, but I'm becoming more worried as the seconds tick by.

"What did you do?"

"Huh? What are you talking about? I didn't do anything."

His eyes narrow. "You did something and now we are the laughing stock of Pittsburgh. With social media, I'm sure the news will travel globally by the end of the day."

I hate when he's mad at me, especially when I don't know how to fix it because I don't even know what I did. I trace back my memories to the last time I saw him which was Friday night. When I left his house, we were happy, so I have no clue what I've done to change the energy between us since then. "I'm not following you. What's going on? Why would people be laughing at us?"

He peers at me quizzically. "You really don't know, do you?" He then shakes his head as if disappointed, and tosses whatever is in his hand at my feet. "Take a look at that."

I bend down and pick up what I quickly realize is the new edition of the *Pittsburgh Star*. Once again, the engagement photo of Andy and me is on the cover.

"I told you about this. Why are they running the same story again?"

"Turn to page twelve," he insists.

I turn the crumpled magazine to the twelfth page and my stomach drops. There's a zoomed in picture of my hand with the fake ring on from Sunday's dinner. *How did they get this picture?* I look up at Andy who's fuming. Speechless, I glance back down at the magazine and read the headline:

STEELERS KICKER ANDY TATE GIVES FIANCÉE A CUBIC
ZIRCONIA

The article goes on to state that I was spotted wearing a big diamond, but upon further investigation, the ring is found to be a phony. It also says that an unnamed family member of mine confirmed that this is the ring given to me by Andy, and that I revealed the ring to the person and other relatives at a recent family gathering. I've been feeling hopeful about the direction of my life this week until now. The *Pittsburgh Star* strikes again, once again ripping my world apart with a feature story on me. But this time it's not Delia dishing the scoop, it's Andy.

I. Am. Mortified. But I'm not alone. Andy is still standing in the middle of my living room with a look on his face that could frighten little children—and me. I know he wants answers, and he wants them now.

"I . . ."

There's nothing I can say to explain. I messed up.

"Where did you get a ring from, Shawna, and why are you pretending that it's your engagement ring?"

A tear slides down my face. I feel like I've been framed, but I did this to myself, so it's hard to cry foul. "This story is not completely true."

He takes a few steps closer to me and points at the magazine. "Is this or isn't this a picture of you wearing a ring that looks like an engagement ring?"

"Yes, it's me. It's just some costume jewelry that I bought," I try to explain. I know that I'm busted, but there's no need to confess to Andy exactly what I did, right? "I wear costume jewelry all of the time. You know that," I say instead, hoping it will appease him.

He doesn't cool down. "But I've never seen this ring. Not only that, but you're telling people this is the ring I purchased for you."

"This is just a misunderstanding. I bought the ring not too long ago, and when I went over to my parents' house, my family assumed that it was my engagement ring. I never told them that it was."

"But you never refuted it either, did you?" he asks, rhetorically. "You knew that they thought I had given you this ring, and you let them believe it instead of correcting them. You're to blame for the misunderstanding. Why would you wear a ring like that right now when you know people are asking about your engagement ring?"

He's talking to me harshly which hurts my feelings. I'm not the only one to blame. He's also at fault for not giving me a decent proposal. "Because you still haven't bought me one!" I don't mean to let the truth come out, but it spills from me before I can stop it.

He glares at me with a crazed look in his eyes. "That's what this is all about, isn't it? I asked you to have a little patience and you go out and do your own thing. Is this how you're going to act when we get married? Tell me now, so I'll know what to expect!"

"Andy, it's not like that," I cry. "I never wanted this to happen."

He sees me crying and lowers his voice. "Well, it has happened and now we have to deal with it. Get dressed," he demands.

I wipe my eyes. "What? Why?"

He sinks down onto the couch and cradles his face with his hands. "I can't have the entire world thinking I'm a cheapskate who buys my wife-to-be cubic zirconia when I make over a million dollars a year. I wanted to wait until my finances were straight, but you've left me no choice. We're going ring shopping."

Ring Shopping

We travel nearly two hours outside of Pittsburgh to a jewelry store in Altoona, Pennsylvania. Andy is concerned that if we shop for a ring locally that the *Pittsburgh Star* reporters will have a new story for their next week's edition. The tension between us can be felt throughout the entire ride. He doesn't speak to me, instead he turns up the volume on his car stereo and allows *The Walls Group,* a family gospel group, to entertain us during the drive. I feel guilty because I know the finger of blame really points at me. I never meant to hurt Andy's reputation or make him feel forced to buy me an expensive ring. Our trip to the jewelry store should be an exciting experience for the both of us, not a covert operation to satisfy the opinion of the public.

When I step into the jewelry store, I feel like I'm in heaven and hell at the same time. An array of spectacular gems shine from beneath the glass cases, drawing me to gaze at each of them in delight. Alternatively, the moment we walk inside, Andy struts over to the far corner of the room, folds his arms, and stares at me like he works security for the jeweler and suspects me as a thief. The sales associates seem baffled by our behavior, and one of them walks over to Andy and asks if she can help him.

"No, I'm fine, but you can help her. She's looking for an engagement ring—a big one. Money is no option. Just give her whatever she wants," he says sarcastically.

I'm hurt and offended. If I wasn't a Christian, I would test him and try to buy the most expensive piece in the store, but I've already caused enough commotion for one day, so I purse my lips and will myself to be quiet.

The sales associate, most likely unsure of how to respond to Andy, leaves his side and comes over to me. "How can I help you, ma'am?" she says politely.

"Like he said, I need an engagement ring. Please, show me what you have."

The woman spends the next hour showing me rings and letting me try them on. I fall in love with a 5.10 carat, princess cut diamond ring, set in a platinum, French Halo "V" band. The instant I slide it on my ring finger, I know it's the one. It fits perfectly and wouldn't have to be resized, but I'm hesitant on admitting how much I want it. I peak at the price on the ring. It's slightly less than $100,000.

While I'm trying it on, Andy leaves his position near the wall and comes over to me. When I feel him close, I begin to remove the ring from my finger, not wanting to let on that I'm diamond struck.

"You like that one, don't you?" he asks. He figures it out anyway.

"It's very nice, but they're all nice. They're diamonds," I say.

"But you reacted differently to that one. I can see it in your eyes," he persists.

"Whatever," I say, handing the ring back to the sales associate.

"How much is it?" he asks me.

"I don't know," I lie. I really don't know why I can't seem to be honest with him about this ring thing. I guess it's knowing that he doesn't want to spend so much money right now that makes it difficult for me to just say exactly what I want.

"Ma'am," Andy says to the saleslady. "How much is the ring?"

"Ninety-five thousand dollars, but we're having a 10 percent off sale today for any purchase over $5,000, so you'd save about $9,500," she says eagerly, glancing between the both of us. She hasn't recognized him as a star athlete so I'm sure she's wondering if we can even afford jewelry this pricey. Technically, I can't afford it, but Mr. NFL could buy a few of these rings without blinking—which fuels the annoyance inside of me about why he didn't just buy the ring in the first place.

Andy looks at me with a blank expression. I hate when he does that. "Shawna, do you want the ring?"

For the sake of being difficult, I want to say no, but my love for the doggone thing won't let me. Instead, I reply, "Whatever. It's your money."

He cuts his eyes and me and says to the associate, "We'll take the ring. Please put the ring box in a bag, but let her wear the ring out of the store."

I've never seen Andy be so authoritative. Did I create this monster?

Shattered Dreams

It's now Monday evening, and I'm flying first class to Miami for a week of training. I look down at the brilliant diamond ring on my left finger and feel so completely torn. My dreams have finally come true. I'm engaged to Andy and I have a $100,000 ring to prove it. Nevertheless, my strained relationship with the man that I love causes this exciting time to feel bittersweet.

I've been wearing the ring nonstop since Andy purchased it for me on Saturday. Karima was right—I can't take the doggone thing off. It's so lovely and expensive that I can't fathom removing it from my hand or presence. Despite my obsession with the jewel, I'm sad that Andy's acting distant. He didn't say much to me during the drive home, he didn't call me before or after his game yesterday, and he didn't even stop by to see me before I left for the airport today. Honestly, I'm surprised he even bought the ring for me and still wants to get married. My dreams of being the quintessential wife are shattering before my very eyes.

I get to my hotel room late, take a shower, and go straight to bed. By 9:00 a.m., I am having breakfast with Diana at *Edge, Steak & Bar*, the hotel's American cuisine restaurant, located on the 7th floor.

"I've heard about your recent news cover stories," she says with a polite smile.

Before we get too deep into work-related business, she gets a little personal. I wondered if the news would travel to Diana. Evidently it has. "That's not the news. That's tabloids," I say.

"Point taken," she says then looks down at my ring that shimmers against the Florida sun, which pours in from the floor to ceiling windows. "Impressive ring. I see that the tabloids were wrong about you. Did they Photoshop a fake ring on your hand or something?"

"No, just a misunderstanding," I say. Being my direct supervisor, my public persona reflects both her and the company. She deserves an explanation and I give her one. "I wasn't wearing my ring at the time and they confused some costume jewelry I have with the real deal. Always looking for a story, I guess."

She nods. "I guess you're right. Well, I'm glad you were able to resolve the matter. It's none of my business, but I'd hate to see your fiancé's celebrity status distract you as you start this new position."

I fold my hands in front of me. "I understand and it won't be a problem. My mind is focused and I'm ready to rock and roll."

"Excellent," she says.

I wish that were true.

By the time I return to Pittsburgh on Saturday, I'm jetlagged and semi-depressed. Being away from Andy for an entire week is awful, especially since he's barely speaking to me. I called him a few times while I was in Florida, but he either didn't answer his phone or was short with me when he did. It's safe to say that he's still upset with me. He hasn't mentioned calling off the engagement, but with the way he's been acting, I'm certain he's thought about it. I go over the situation in my mind a thousand times trying to figure out where I went wrong. Yes, maybe I was too focused on getting a ring and having the perfect engagement story, but that was the way I always imagined the situation would unfold. I never once considered the idea that getting engaged might not be an epic tale, but instead just an agreement between two people that want to be together.

I realize that I've allowed my own selfish expectations and the pressure from those around me to cloud what I thought about Andy and the way he proposed. I'm not saying that he couldn't have done a better job, but I shouldn't have said yes if I wasn't okay with the way the matter was handled. I haven't been honest at all with him over the past several weeks, and because of that, the ugly results rest on my shoulders.

Of course, my mother finds out about the recent article in the *Pittsburgh Star* and has been calling me all week about it. After ignoring the first five attempts she makes, I take her sixth call, tolerating about ten minutes of fusing over my refusal to talk to her and how much I've embarrassed her with my fake ring. Aunt Wanda has been using it to belittle her ever since. To get my mom off my back, I snap a picture of my real ring and text message it to her. I'm sure she immediately forwarded the picture to Aunt Wanda and Vanessa, earning back her title as the winner. Good grief!

Delia also picked up another three copies of the issue with my faux ring.

"Why would you attempt a fake-out like that?" she asks me once she finally gets a hold of me by phone. "People know diamonds, especially rich women and tabloids. You should have known it was going to blow up in your face."

I hate when folks kick you while you're already down. As much as I love both my mother and my best friend, I'm ready to pull away from the both of them and become one with my husband-to-be, if he'll still have me. At some point in growing up, we get to the point where the relationships that matter most are the ones where people accept us for who we really are and respect our boundaries. If we're blessed, we get that kind of person in our mate. Andy may not be perfect, but he gives me my space to grow and become the person I need to be for me. That's more than I can say for my mom and Delia.

Saturday evening, there's a knock on my door—it's a surprise house visit from my father. He rarely comes to see me, but when he does, I'm grateful to know that he's thinking of me.

"You know you're driving your mother crazy, who's then driving me crazy," he says.

I lean my head on his shoulder. "I'm sorry, Daddy. Sometimes I wish she would stop trying to run my life. When will she accept that I'm an adult and I don't need her telling me what to do?"

He rubs my hair gently like he used to do when I was a child. "She'll stop meddling in your life when you start acting like an adult."

I sit up. "Daddy! Are you trying to say I'm immature?"

"No, you've always been mature, but you're so used to your mother dominating you that you don't stand up for yourself. People will push you only as far as you let them—your mother included."

I sigh. "I try to stand up to her, but she's so aggressive."

"And you're so passive-aggressive," he says then chuckles. "You've always been like that. If you don't like something, instead of confronting the person and just being honest, you run around doing little sneaky things to get the person back."

I frown. "When do I do that?"

"All the time. Your mom calls you and you ignore her call. Just answer the phone and tell her you don't want to hear it. That's what I do when she starts getting on my nerves. I'm used to her, but even I can only take so much. She doesn't like to be told no, but she has to respect my request."

My dad has me pegged. I can't even deny it. "You make it sound so simple. I just don't want to hurt anyone's feelings."

"It is that simple," he says. "It's not about you salvaging other feelings; it's about you being scared of conflict. Baby girl, conflict is a part of life. Everyone won't like everything you say, but if they love you, they'll listen. Don't miss out on giving people a chance to love you for who you really are and not who they think you are because you're not being yourself. Tell people the truth so that they can know you the way I know you. You are an exquisite woman, and those who deserve to be in your life can handle your honesty."

Telling the Truth

My daddy's words resonate with me. He's right. I am very passive-aggressive and I avoid conflict at all costs. I haven't been truthful with the people closest to me because I feared their rejection and judgment. I haven't been upfront with Andy because I didn't want him to leave me. The ironic part is that not telling him the truth has caused more damage than just saying what is on my heart and mind.

Tuesday, I go to see Andy. It's time for me to make things right between us. There's no point in continuing in our engagement if we're not going to sit down like adults and work through the messy stuff.

"We need to talk," I say as I have a seat across from him at his dining room table. I usually avoid saying this to him. I know that men hate those four words—we need to talk—but it's time for me to stop pretending to be the perfect woman and just be a woman, plain and simple.

"I agree," he says, looking at me with sad eyes.

I take a deep breath in and begin my confession. "Andy, first let me apologize. I haven't told you the truth for a while now. I thought that bottling it up inside and just going along with what you wanted was the right thing to do. Now I see that I should have just talked to you about how I was feeling instead of acting like things were okay.

"When we agreed to get married that night in Miami, I was very disappointed. I wanted to marry you, but I also wanted a romantic proposal, not just, 'Okay, let's get married.' I wanted you to want me as your bride so much that you planned out a nice dinner or some sweet activity, followed by you getting down on one knee and asking me to be your wife. I wanted a proposal with a ring and a thrilling story that I could share over and over again throughout the years of our marriage.

"What's funny is I did get the thrilling story, but not in the way I imagined. When you didn't give me the proposal of my dreams, I should have just requested that you propose to me the right way—or at least the way I wanted—instead of agreeing and then being resentful about it. I understood your dilemma with buying the ring, but that didn't change the amount of pressure I felt from others to have a ring on my finger, or my own desire to wear a symbol of our commitment. I should have told you that too instead of buying a fake ring or saying it was okay for me not to have one at all. I've made so many mistakes over the past several weeks, but the one thing I did get right was agreeing to marry you. You are everything I could have ever asked for in a man, and although you don't always see life the way I see it, you challenge me to be the very best that I can be. I hope that it's not too late for us to rewind time and give our engagement another try."

The entire time I've been talking, he's been making eye contact with me. I look away from him, uneasy about how he'll react to my speech. Despite his previous estrangement from me, he reaches across the table and grabs my hand, squeezing it affectionately.

"Of course, it's not too late," he finally says. "Thank you for finally telling me how you really feel. I'm sorry that this engagement has been so difficult for you. I guess I never thought about it from your perspective. You're right; I should have given you a more well thought out proposal, but I called myself being spontaneous and going with the flow. And I'm sorry if my financial planning got in the way of you having a symbol of our commitment. I just wanted us to have the provisions we need for the future."

I reach into my purse and pull out the ring box that came with my engagement ring. Carefully, I slide the ring off my finger and place it inside the box. I then put the box on the table and slide it over to him.

He looks confused. "What are you doing? Are you breaking up with me?"

I laugh. "No, not at all. I don't need that ring to be engaged to you. I know that having a secure financial future for us is what's important to you, and it's also what's important to me too. I was being foolish when I asked for such an expensive ring. I think we should forget the ring and focus on building our lives together."

He tries to push the box back in my direction. "But I bought it for you."

I return the box back to his side of the table. "I know and I appreciate it. But I want you to take it back and put that money back into your account."

"Don't you want an engagement ring?" he asks.

I nod. "I do, but maybe we can get something cheaper. Let's say $2,000?"

"Are you sure?"

"Yes, I'm sure. A $100,000 ring doesn't tell me that you love me any more than a $2,000 one. It's the thought and the man behind the ring that matters most."

He stands up and walks over to my side of the table, scooping me up into his arms.

"I truly am one lucky man," he says before kissing me softly.

"Not lucky, blessed," I say when we come up for air.

Epilogue

Mr. & Mrs. Andy Tate

In my past dreams, my wedding is an expensive affair, filled with affluent people, costly wine, and a to-die-for wedding dress. But today, in reality, my wedding is quaint, affordable, simple, yet beautiful. We decide to have a destination wedding, rolling the cost of both the wedding and the honeymoon into one. It's not that Andy and I can't swing the fee for a traditional wedding, but with many changes that have occurred within our lives—including him retiring from football—being economical makes more sense. We both feel more at ease having a large savings account rather than spending frivolously on a large wedding.

In the past several months, we've both made adjustments for our new lives together. Andy is going back to school for finance and is in the process of starting a business teaching professional athletes how to manage their money and prepare for retirement. He already has a handful of clients, mostly former teammates. I'm sure once he finishes his degree and gets a few testimonials from those he is currently working with, his business will grow substantially.

I've been really enjoying my position as a regional cosmetics manager. I never thought that I wanted a career, but helping women to feel good about themselves makes me feel good about myself. I've worked out a schedule with Diana to work from home three out of five days a week unless I'm traveling. We've also agreed that once Andy and I start having children, I'll decrease my number of travel days and be able to telecommute instead. Upon my recommendation, Delia is now the cosmetics manager for my old store, filling my former position. I've been working closely with her to bring her up to speed with the job, and grooming her so that she too can eventually be promoted to the regional level. Diana plans to retire in the next five to ten years. Who knows? Maybe by then I'll be ready to take over her role. Director of Cosmetics has a nice ring to it.

Speaking of ring, I do finally get mine—and I must admit, it was well worth the wait. While making up, Andy and I agreed to purchase a less expensive engagement ring. After all of the fuss I made over getting a diamond, I feel it was only fair that I get over the materialistic and superficial aspect of having a gaudy ring, and appreciate what the ring actually symbolizes. In the process, I learn that love and marriage has nothing to do with how much bling adorns my left hand. I want the man, the partner, the lifetime companion much more than I want a piece of jewelry. Plenty of people have flashy rocks, but their homes are loveless—what's the point of having the ring without the love?

At our wedding ceremony in Cabo San Lucas, Mexico, Andy makes me the happiest woman in the world. Not only does he become my husband, finally giving me my lifelong dream title of wife, he also gives me two rings—a wedding band and a second engagement ring. The 5-carat engagement ring that I gave back!

"I don't understand," I say to him, completely overwhelmed by the ostentatious diamond. "I thought we were going to bypass on this ring. I'm okay with the one I already have."

He smiles. "Babe, I always planned to give you a big diamond, I just needed the timing to be right. You've sacrificed so much by giving up your dream wedding and have been so supportive of the changes in my life and career. I just wanted—no I needed—to show you just how much I love you and I appreciate all that you do for me."

I look down at the sparkling diamond that he has placed on my finger along with the diamond wedding band. "If this is going to eat too much into our savings, we can take it back. It's beautiful and I love it, but I want what's best for us so much more. That is what's most important to me. I'm sorry I ever made you feel like I needed any more to love you."

"The ring is yours," he assures me. "I promised you that I would give you the ring you wanted with no debt attached, and I keep my promises. Just like I intend to keep my promise to love you and stand by your side through all of the ups and downs of life, till death do us part."

I want to kiss him, but I look up and realize that the minister and our wedding guests are watching our entire interaction, waiting for our moment to end so that we can continue with the ceremony.

"Sorry," I say to the preacher. "You can continue."

The preacher grins. "I think you two have said all that needs to be said. By the power vested in me, I pronounce you husband and wife. You may kiss your bride."

Andy pulls me close and kisses me softly. When he pulls away, I'm sure that he'll keep all of his promises to me.

"Ladies and gentlemen," the preacher says, "I introduce for the first time, Mr. and Mrs. Andy Tate."

Our guests stand and applaud. We turn to face them, but before we walk back down the aisle, I take a quick moment for myself and put out my left hand for the crowd to see.

I'm now a wife with three rings!

Wife Insurance

Wealthy resort owner, Cole Haven, is supposed to get married on Christmas to Violet, the woman he's been engaged to for the past five years. Yet, the same problem that has kept him from committing to the ceremony once again gives him an impossible case of cold feet— his distrust for women due to the actions of his ex-wife, Sophia. When Sophia hits him with an unreasonable ultimatum a month before his holiday wedding, and Violet is unwilling to compromise this Christmas, Cole will have to choose between taking a leap of faith or using the past as an indicator for what the future holds. If only he had a bit of wife insurance to guarantee him that marriage to Violet won't be the second biggest mistake of his life…

Wife Next Door

Felicia Jefferson and Morris Bryson have been best friends since childhood. Morris has always appreciated Felicia for standing by his side through his bouts with a lifelong disease. At age 16, they made a pact that if neither of them were married by the time she turned 35, they would marry one another. As fate would have it, at 36, his chronic illness worsens and he attempts to cash-in on his agreement with Felicia, wanting to experience marriage before he dies. As much as Felicia desires to grant her sick friend's request, marrying Morris means breaking up with her boyfriend of two years and sacrificing her plans to marry for love. Is a lifetime of friendship strong enough to survive an unexpected proposal, sympathy marriage, and a life-threatening disease?

About the Author

A'ndrea J. Wilson is the author of over twenty books, including the award-winning Wife 101 series. A'ndrea dates her writing career back to high school where she majored in creative writing at Rochester, New York's School of the Arts. After graduation, she pursued careers in psychology and education, earning a Master's degree in Marriage and Family Counseling and a Ph.D. in Educational Leadership. An avid reader, she could never shake her passion for books, which eventually led to her penning her first manuscript. Her continuously growing body of faith-based work primarily focuses on integrating her clinical background and interest in relationship development with fiction; however, she also writes supernatural thrillers under the pseudonym Janell. In addition to writing, A'ndrea is a college professor and the president of Divine Garden Press, an independent publishing company based in Georgia. For more information, please visit her at www.andreawilsononline.com or www.wife101.com.

www.ingramcontent.com/pod-product-compliance
Lightning Source LLC
Chambersburg PA
CBHW020630130626
46552CB00003B/1157